Meet
Jacqueline Kennedy Onassis

by Anne Capeci

A Bullseye Biography

Random House 🏠 **New York**

Photo credits: AP/Wide World Photos, p. 4, 66, 76; The Bettmann Archive, p. 20; Ted Lyson, p. 84, 85; Reuters/Bettmann, p. 88, 91; UPI/Bettmann, p. 11, 13, 14, 30, 33, 35, 45, 46, 49, 64, 71, 81, 93.

A BULLSEYE BOOK PUBLISHED BY RANDOM HOUSE, INC.

Cover design by Fabia Wargin Design and Creative Media Applications, Inc.
Copyright © 1995 by Anne Capeci
All rights reserved under International and Pan-American Copyright Conventions.
Published in the United States by Random House, Inc., New York, and simultaneously in Canada by Random House of Canada Limited, Toronto.

Library of Congress Cataloging-in-Publication Data:
Capeci, Anne. Meet Jacqueline Kennedy Onassis / by Anne Capeci. p. cm.—
(A Bullseye biography) ISBN 0-679-87184-5 (pbk.) 1. Onassis, Jacqueline Kennedy, 1929–1994—Juvenile literature. 2. Celebrities—United States—Biography—Juvenile literature. 3. Presidents' spouses—United States—Biography—Juvenile literature.
4. United States—Biography—Juvenile literature. I. Title. II. Series.
CT275.O552C36 1995 973.922'092—dc20 [B] 94-30191

Manufactured in the United States of America 10 9 8 7 6 5 4 3 2 1

Contents

*Jackie, Caroline, and John Jr. say good-bye
to their husband and father.*

I

"They've Killed Jack!"

It is late November, 1963. A woman dressed all in black stands outside a church in Washington, D.C. A veil covers her face. She is holding the hands of her two young children, Caroline and John Jr. The woman's name is Jacqueline Bouvier Kennedy, and this is a very sad day for her. It is the day her husband will be buried.

Jacqueline stands very straight as her husband's coffin is carried from the church. She does not cry. When the coffin passes in front of her, she quietly whispers to her three-year-old son, "John, you can salute Daddy now, and say good-bye to him." John Jr. raises his hand in a firm salute. People around the world are watching the funeral on television. They cry when they see such a little boy acting so bravely.

Jacqueline's husband was a very important man. He was John Fitzgerald Kennedy, the 35th president of the United States. President Kennedy worked hard for his country. He wanted to make sure all people in the United States had the same rights and opportunities. He struggled to keep peace in the world. President Kennedy was very popular, but not everyone agreed with the changes he wanted to make. On November 22, 1963, the president was shot and killed by a man named Lee Harvey Oswald.

Jackie, as everyone called Jacqueline, was sitting next to the president when he was shot. They were riding in an open car through the streets of Dallas, Texas. People had come from all over to cheer President Kennedy and his beautiful wife. When the shots rang out, Jackie cried, "They've killed Jack! They've killed my husband—Jack, Jack!" It was a terrifying moment.

There were blood stains on the pink suit that Jackie wore, but she would not change her clothes. She wanted Americans to see the blood. She thought it would help them to understand this awful tragedy.

During the next few days, Jackie proved that she was a very strong and brave woman. She insisted on taking care of every detail of her husband's funeral herself.

Nearly one hundred years earlier, President Abraham Lincoln had been shot and killed. At President Lincoln's funeral, there had been a horse without a rider, to show people that a brave soldier had fallen. Jackie decided to have a riderless horse at President Kennedy's funeral, too. She chose to bury the president at Arlington National Cemetery, alongside others who had died for their country. She arranged to have a flame lit above his grave that would never go out. She wanted to show that John Kennedy's spirit would shine forever. She also made special cards to give to the leaders from around the world who came to honor her husband at his funeral. The cards read: "Dear God, please take care of your servant John Fitzgerald Kennedy."

Jackie worked day and night preparing for the funeral. She hardly slept or ate. No matter how sad she felt, she never cried in public. People across the country mourned the president's death. They were impressed by Jackie's courage and strength.

Jackie did not know what would happen to her and her children now. She was not even sure where she and Caroline and John Jr. would live. But the one thing she did know was that her life—and the nation's spirit—would never be the same again.

2
A Girl Named Jackie

Jacqueline Bouvier was born on July 28, 1929, in Southampton, Long Island, near New York City. Jackie's father was named John V. Bouvier III. He was a stockbroker. Her mother, Janet Lee Bouvier, was a rich and fashionable young New Yorker. Jackie had a younger sister. Her name was Caroline Lee Bouvier, but everyone called her Lee.

Jackie's childhood was very special. Her family lived in an elegant apartment on Park Avenue, in New York City. They had lots

*Jackie and sister Lee play with a dog at the Annual
Dog Show in Easthampton, Long Island.*

of servants. The Bouviers had a big country estate on Long Island, too. It was called Lasata, which is an Indian word that means "place of peace." Jackie and Lee loved spending weekends and summers at Lasata, riding horses and playing games.

As a little girl, Jackie was boisterous and rebellious. She did not like wearing a uniform to Miss Chapin's, the private school she attended. She acted up in class and was often sent to see the headmistress. One of Jackie's classmates told Jackie's mother that Jackie was "the very worst behaved girl in school."

But Jackie was smart, too. She learned how to read before she even started kindergarten! Jackie loved books. Some of her favorites were *The Wizard of Oz*, *Little Lord Fauntleroy*, and *Winnie-the-Pooh*.

By the time she was eight years old, Jackie had started writing her own stories. One story was about the family's pet terrier. It was called "The Adventures of George Woofty, Esq." Jackie also liked to sketch. Sometimes she decorated her stories with drawings.

But Jackie's favorite hobby was horseback riding. Her mother put her on a pony for the first time when she was just a year old! Jackie was a fast learner, and she had a lot of

Jackie leads her pony at a horse show.

pluck. If a horse threw her, she always climbed back on.

The Bouviers owned seven horses. One of them was a beautiful chestnut show horse named Danseuse. Danseuse is French for

John and Janet Bouvier meet young Jackie after riding.

"Dancer." Jackie's mother decided to give Danseuse to Jackie. For hours every day Jackie would exercise her horse. Riding Danseuse, she competed in horse shows all around Long Island. Jackie loved riding in the shows. She and Danseuse often won.

14

Before long, she had a big collection of blue ribbons.

Jackie's mother and father tried to give their daughters everything little girls could want. Jackie and Lee had pretty clothes and horses to ride. They went to the best schools. They had lots of toys and pets. But their family life wasn't always happy. As Jackie and Lee grew older, their parents argued more and more.

When Jackie was seven years old, her parents decided not to live together anymore. Jackie and Lee stayed with their mother. Their father moved nearby and visited them on weekends.

John Bouvier's nickname was Black Jack, because he had shiny black hair and a dark mustache. He was handsome and dashing. Everyone said that Jackie looked a lot like Jack. She had the same dark hair, wide-set eyes, and good looks.

The girls were especially close to their father. Jackie and Lee did lots of fun things with Jack when they saw him. Jack took his daughters to the zoo and bought them ice cream sodas. He took them for horse-and-buggy rides through Central Park. He gave them a tour of the New York Stock Exchange. Jackie always looked forward to her visits with her father.

When Jackie was 11 years old, Jack and Janet Bouvier were divorced. Jackie kept doing the same things she had always done. She went to school. She read more than ever and competed in horse shows.

But being away from her father was hard for Jackie. She became moody and quiet. She spent a lot of time alone. On the surface, Jackie seemed to have everything. But deep down, her life was not at all perfect.

3

A New Life

When Jackie was 15, she entered Miss Porter's School. Miss Porter's is an exclusive all-girls boarding school in Farmington, Connecticut.

Miss Porter's offered a fine education. It also taught young girls how to behave in the small and special world they would live in when they grew up. This world of rich, powerful, and fashionable people was often called "society."

Jackie and her classmates learned how to

dress, talk, and act properly in society. Every Friday afternoon, they had to attend a formal tea with their teachers. The girls at Miss Porter's were not allowed to play cards or smoke. They were not allowed to read popular romance novels either. Those things were not considered proper for young women like themselves.

Jackie did not like having to obey so many rules. She stole cookies from the school kitchen. She wore hairstyles and makeup that her teachers thought were too daring. Jackie was very independent. She liked to create her own style instead of following the trends that were popular with her classmates.

By now, Jackie's mother had remarried. Janet's new husband was Hugh Dudley Auchincloss. Jackie and Lee called him "Uncle Hughdie." Uncle Hughdie had three children of his own. They were Yusha, Nina, and Thomas. Before long, Jackie's mother and Hugh had two more children, a daughter named Janet and a son named Jamie. Now Jackie and Lee had five new brothers and sisters!

Hugh Auchincloss was a financier. A financier is someone who makes and invests big sums of money for himself and other people. Hugh owned two big estates. His main home was in McLean, Virginia, near Washington, D.C. It was called Merrywood. His second home, Hammersmith Farm, was in Newport, Rhode Island. When Jackie was on vacation from Miss Porter's, she spent time with her new family both at Merrywood and at Hammersmith Farm. She and Lee also visited their father at Lasata and at his apartment in New York City.

In the spring of 1947, Jackie was ready to graduate from Miss Porter's. She was also

Jackie, with her father, at Belmont Park Race Track.

preparing for another very important event, her Coming Out party. At the age of 18, Jackie was ready to be introduced to important people in society. At the party, she would make her "debut," her first formal appearance as an adult.

Jackie decided to have her Coming Out party at Hammersmith Farm. Her mother and Uncle Hughdie planned an afternoon tea and dance. There was a formal dinner, too. It was a very big event—three hundred people came!

Jackie chose the dress for her Coming Out party very carefully. Debutantes, as the young ladies were called, often wore expensive dresses that were made for them by famous designers. Jackie decided to wear something much simpler. Her dress was white, with a full skirt and white roses around the neckline. It wasn't expensive. It wasn't made by anyone famous. But everyone agreed that Jackie looked very beautiful.

Jackie made a big impression at her Coming Out. Everyone thought that she was pretty and smart. She had a special style that made people notice her. One reporter wrote that Jackie had "the looks of a fairy-tale princess." Jackie made such a big splash that an important society reporter named her the Number One Debutante of the Year.

People began paying even more attention to Jackie. Newspapers wanted to interview her and take her picture. Young men wanted to date her.

Jackie wasn't used to having such a fuss made over her. She was very private. She liked to ask other people about themselves but didn't like to talk about herself.

Little did Jackie know that people all around the world would be paying attention to her for the rest of her life.

4

Off to College!

In the fall of 1947, Jackie entered Vassar College, in Poughkeepsie, New York. It was a demanding school, and Jackie worked hard. She especially liked to study the plays of William Shakespeare, the great English writer.

Vassar College rewarded students who did well. When students earned very good grades, their names were placed on a list called the dean's list. Jackie made the dean's list, but she never bragged about how well she did.

After two years at Vassar, Jackie decided to spend a year studying in Paris, France. She had made friends with a French girl named Claude de Renty. Claude and her mother lived in Paris. They invited Jackie to stay with them while she was in France.

Jackie loved Paris. When she wasn't going to classes, she explored the city. She went to museums, the ballet, and the opera. Sometimes she sat in sidewalk cafes and watched people go by. Often she walked along the Seine River.

She enjoyed traveling outside of Paris, too. Jackie and Claude drove all over France. Jackie's mother and Uncle Hughdie took her on a trip to Austria and Germany. Jackie also traveled to Ireland and Scotland with her brother Yusha.

Afterward, Jackie came home to the United States. But she would always remember the time she spent in France. She once said that it was her "happiest and most carefree year."

Jackie decided not to return to Vassar. Instead, she chose to finish college at George Washington University, in Washington, D.C. Jackie had studied French literature while she was in Paris. She chose that subject as her major at George Washington University.

Before Jackie graduated, she competed in a writing contest. Everyone who entered had to write an essay on "People I Wish I Had Known." More than 1,200 college students entered the contest.

Jackie wrote about three people she wished she had known. One of them was a French poet named Charles Baudelaire, who lived in the 1800s. The second was an English writer, Oscar Wilde. He wrote in the late 1800s. The third person Jackie wrote about was Sergei Diaghilev, a Russian man who started a very important ballet company in Paris in 1909.

All of Jackie's hard work paid off. She won the contest!

Part of her prize was to spend six months working in the Paris office of *Vogue*, a famous fashion magazine. Jackie was excited about the prize. But her mother and Hugh Auchincloss did not want Jackie to go back to Paris. They were afraid that she would have so much fun that she would never return to the United States!

Jackie's mother and Uncle Hughdie made a deal with Jackie. If she would agree not to accept the prize, they would send her and Lee to Europe for the summer. The two girls traveled to England, France, Italy, and Spain. They made a scrapbook of their trip, with drawings and rhymes and stories about all the places they visited and the people they met. When they returned home at the end of the summer, they gave the scrapbook to their mother.

Jackie was now 21 years old. She had graduated from George Washington University. Her whole life was ahead of her. It was exciting for Jackie to think about what she would do next.

5

An Inquiring Photographer

Jackie was not sure what kind of work she wanted to do, or where she wanted to live. Her father wanted her to live with him in New York City. He told Jackie that he would give her a job at his company. Jackie's mother wanted her to live at Merrywood, near Washington, D.C. She thought that Jackie could find a better job there than in New York.

Jackie decided to stay in Washington. She got a job working on a newspaper called the *Washington Times-Herald*. At first, Jackie helped out by doing odd jobs around the office. When people wanted coffee, Jackie got it for them. She answered phones and ran errands.

Jackie knew that she could handle more important work. Before long, she convinced the newspaper's chief editor, Frank Waldrop, to give her a bigger job.

The *Times-Herald* was starting a new feature in their paper. It was called the Inquiring Photographer. Mr. Waldrop thought that Jackie was right for the job.

Every day, Jackie interviewed people on the streets of the city. She asked them questions and took their pictures. Then she published their comments and photographs in the *Times-Herald*.

Jackie on the job as Inquiring Photographer in Washington, D.C.

Being Inquiring Photographer was not easy. Jackie found it hard to use the big, bulky camera that newspaper photographers worked with. She had to work quickly in order to finish her column on time every day. Before long, Jackie got the hang of it.

She thought up funny questions to ask: "Are men braver than women in the dental chair?" "If you were going to be executed tomorrow morning, what would you order for your last meal on earth?" To children, "Why don't Santa's reindeer come down the chimney?" She was a great success!

Before starting her job at the *Washington Times-Herald*, Jackie had met a young man named John Husted. John was a banker who lived in New York City. He and Jackie began dating. They spent a lot of time together. On a snowy winter night near the end of 1951, John and Jackie decided to get engaged.

Jackie and John made plans to marry in June of 1952. But early in 1952, Jackie changed her mind.

Jackie had met a different man, and she had fallen in love with him!

The man's name was John Fitzgerald

Kennedy. Most people called him Jack. He was a politician from Boston, Massachusetts, who wanted to become a United States senator. A U.S. senator represents the people from his state. He works in Washington, D.C., to help create laws that he thinks will be good for the country and for the people he represents.

Jackie liked the handsome young politician. Jack had been a hero when he was in the Navy during World War II. He had helped to save the lives of his crew after their boat was hit by a Japanese destroyer. He was smart. He liked to make witty jokes, just as Jackie did. Jack and Jackie had the same religious background, too. They both came from Roman Catholic families.

Jack Kennedy came from a very big family. He had two brothers and four sisters! The Kennedys were lively and noisy. They

Recently engaged, John and Jackie share a view
from the Kennedy's Hyannisport home.

loved to talk and joke around. They competed with one another in all sorts of games
and sports. Sometimes they played tennis or
touch football. Other times they had sailing
races or played softball.

Jackie sometimes played along with Jack and his brothers and sisters. It wasn't always easy. During one touch football game, she even broke her ankle! Once, she joked to a friend, "I don't know if I'll live long enough to marry Jack."

Sometimes it was hard for Jackie and Jack to find time to spend together. They both traveled a lot. Jack was elected senator in 1952. He moved to Washington, but he still spent a lot of time in Massachusetts. When Jack Kennedy decided to ask Jackie to marry him, she was in London. He had to send her a telegram to propose!

Jackie's answer was yes, and on September 12, 1953, Jacqueline Bouvier and John F. Kennedy were married. The reception was at Hammersmith Farm. There were so many guests that it took the bride and groom two and a half hours to greet them all!

A beautiful bride.

The day was almost perfect, except for one thing. Jackie's father, Jack Bouvier, was not able to attend her wedding. Uncle Hughdie walked Jackie down the aisle instead. Jackie was disappointed, but she kept her feelings to herself. Everyone at the wedding saw only a happy, smiling bride.

Jackie looked beautiful in her white wedding gown. She wore a lace veil that had belonged to her grandmother. She danced with her new husband. Together, she and Jack cut their wedding cake. The cake was four feet tall! When the wedding was over, Jack and Jackie left for their honeymoon in Acapulco, a city in Mexico.

Jackie was now Mrs. John F. Kennedy. It was the beginning of a great new adventure.

6

A Wife and a Mother

Jackie wanted to be a good wife to Jack. He was very busy, and he often got sick, but Jackie made sure that he ate well. He needed his strength.

She was proud that the people of Massachusetts had elected him to represent them in the U.S. Senate. She learned as much about Jack's job as she could. Whenever Jack made an important speech in the Senate, Jackie went and listened. She joined a group of senator's wives who raised money for local museums.

John Kennedy worked hard at his job. He had lots of ideas for helping the men and women he represented. And he liked to talk about his ideas.

Jack did not always pay attention to how he looked when he spoke in public. If his suit was wrinkled, or his socks were two different colors, he did not care. Sometimes Jack would slouch and stuff his hands in his pockets when he gave a speech. When he got excited, he spoke too fast. People could not always understand him.

Jackie thought that she could help Jack to make a better impression when he talked to people about his ideas. She told him to stand very straight when he spoke. She helped Jack to speak more slowly and clearly.

She taught him how to use his hands to help make a point. She made sure that his suits were not wrinkled and that his socks always matched.

During hard times, Jackie was there for her husband, too. In 1954, Jack had to have an operation on his back. The operation was very serious. Afterward, it took Jack a long time to get well. Jackie sat with him for hours every day. She read aloud to Jack and gave him silly presents to make him laugh. She played checkers and other games with him.

When he started getting better, Jackie encouraged her husband to read, write, and paint on his own. Jack decided to write a book. He wanted to tell the stories of eight great U.S. senators.

Jackie helped her husband with his new project. Jack still could not get out of bed, so Jackie went to the library to find information he could use in his book. Jack read parts of the book to Jackie and asked her what she thought. He listened to Jackie's advice.

Jack called the book *Profiles in Courage*. Many people wanted to read it. *Profiles in Courage* won a Pulitzer Prize, which is a very high honor.

In his book, Jack thanked Jackie for all her help. He wrote: "This book would not have been possible without the encouragement, assistance and criticisms offered by my wife, Jacqueline."

In 1955, Jack was finally well enough to return to his job in the United States Senate. Jack was excited about his work. In 1956, the people of the United States would elect a new president and vice-president. Jack had already started thinking about that election.

There are two major American political parties. They are the Democratic Party and the Republican Party. Jack belonged to the Democratic Party. Every four years, members from each party have a big meeting, called a convention. Each party chooses a few people from each state to go to its convention. Those people are called delegates. At the convention, the delegates choose someone to run for president of the United States, and someone to run for vice-president. These people represent the party's ideas about how to solve the country's problems.

In 1956, the president was Dwight D. Eisenhower and the vice-president was Richard M. Nixon. They were Republicans. The Republican Party chose them to run again.

Most Democrats wanted a man named Adlai Stevenson to run for president in the 1956 election. It was not clear whom the Democratic delegates would choose to run for vice-president. Jack Kennedy wanted the job. He fought hard to convince the delegates to vote for him.

Jack was only 39 years old. That is young to be vice-president of the United States. But the voters liked Kennedy. He thought he might have a chance.

Jackie went to the Democratic Convention with Jack. She did everything she could to help Jack show people that he would make a good candidate for vice-president— that he could help the party win the election. She talked to Democratic delegates from New England about her husband. She cheered Jack when he gave a speech for Adlai Stevenson.

In the end, the Democratic delegates did not choose Jack Kennedy. They voted for another senator, Estes Kefauver. But Jack came much closer than people thought he would. He missed being chosen by fewer than 31 votes!

After the convention, Jackie was very tired. Helping Jack at the convention had been hard work. And she and Jack were expecting their first child in a month! She went to Hammersmith Farm to rest and wait.

But a week later, Jackie was rushed to the hospital. The baby was born too soon. Doctors tried to save her, but the little girl did not survive.

The Kennedys were very sad to lose their baby daughter. And a year later, in August of 1957, Jackie lost someone else who was very close to her. Jackie's father died. Although they had not seen each other often in the years before his death, Jack Bouvier still thought about his daughter. A nurse who took care of him in the hospital said that his last word was "Jackie."

But 1957 was a happy year for Jackie, too. In March, she found out that she and Jack were expecting another child. On November 27, 1957, a healthy baby girl was born. Jackie and Jack named her Caroline Bouvier Kennedy.

Jackie and Jack adored Caroline. Jack called her Buttons. He said that his little daughter was "as robust as a sumo wrestler." Jackie had the nursery specially decorated for baby Caroline. No matter how busy she was, Jackie always found time to care for her daughter.

In 1958, Jack ran for re-election as senator. Jackie worked hard in Jack's campaign. She spoke to crowds all over Massachusetts about why they should elect Jack to the Senate again.

Jackie spoke three foreign languages: French, Spanish, and Italian. Many of the

Summertime on Cape Cod—the Kennedys read to little Caroline.

people she talked to spoke Spanish or Italian at home. When Jackie met with Hispanic Americans, she talked to them in Spanish.

*Waving to the crowd in New York, Jackie and John
hope for presidential victory (1960).*

When she met with groups of Italian Americans, she talked to them in Italian. It was a sign of respect for their heritages. They were impressed and very pleased.

Wherever she campaigned with Jack, big crowds came to listen. People liked to see John Kennedy's young wife. She was stylish and full of life. Many people thought that Jackie and Jack represented a new age of change.

Jack Kennedy won the election by a great many votes. Three out of every four voters cast their ballot for him! It was a big victory for Jack. People all over the country started talking about young Senator Kennedy.

Soon Jack felt that he was ready for an even bigger job. He decided to run for president of the United States!

7

At Home in the White House

On the evening of January 20, 1961, Jacqueline Kennedy stood with her husband on the steps of the White House. Hours earlier, John F. Kennedy had become the 35th president of the United States. Now he and Jackie were going to attend the first of five formal balls being given in President Kennedy's honor.

Jackie was very proud of her husband. She and Jack had another reason to cele-

The First Family brings home their newest addition, John Jr. (1961).

brate, too. They had a new son. Their baby boy had been born on November 25. His name was John Fitzgerald Kennedy Jr. His father called him John-John.

Jack, Jackie, Caroline, and John-John moved into the White House. Jackie was now the country's First Lady. First Lady is the title given to the president's wife. Jackie was admired by women all across the country. Many of the women wanted to look just like Jackie. They copied her hairstyle. They wore the same kinds of clothes and hats they saw Jackie wearing, too.

Once again, Jackie did not like being the center of attention. But reporters and photographers and tourists wanted to see President Kennedy's family. They stood outside the White House and took pictures of Caroline and John-John playing on the lawn. Secret Service men guarded Jackie and her children 24 hours a day.

Jackie worried that Caroline and John-John would be affected by so much attention. "The world is pouring terrible adoration at the feet of my children," she said. "How can I bring them up normally?"

The first thing Jackie did was to make sure that the White House was a comfortable home for her family. She put a white canopied bed and some rocking horses in Caroline's bedroom. She chose pink-rosebud wallpaper that she thought her daughter would like. John-John's nursery was blue and white. In it, Jackie put his crib and all of his stuffed animals. She even set up a nursery school in the White House for Caroline and 20 other girls and boys.

"I don't want Caroline and John-John to be raised by nurses and Secret Service agents," Jackie said. She spent as much time with her son and daughter as she could. And she made sure they saw their father, too. Even though John Kennedy was president of the United States, Jackie wanted their children to see him as "no different from any other father on the block." Caroline and John-John even played in the Oval Office while their father worked in it.

It took a lot of hard work, but Jackie made a fine home for her family in the White House. Then she thought about other ways she could contribute to her husband's presidency.

8

First Lady

Jackie Kennedy knew the White House was very important to the people of the United States—and the world. The White House is where the president and his family lives and works. It has many rooms that are open to the public. Over a million people visit it every year.

Jackie wanted the public rooms to be very special. She thought they should honor the important people who had shaped our country. She wanted the White House to show the history of the presidency.

Redecorating the White House was a huge project, but Jackie was very excited about it. She searched for furniture that had belonged to some of the earliest American presidents. She found a mirror that had belonged to George Washington. She put up a portrait of Benjamin Franklin from the 1700s. She found dishes and lamps and clocks that had belonged to other presidents. Jackie even found wallpaper that was over 125 years old. Some of the things had been in the dusty White House attic for many years!

Jackie had a guidebook written for visitors to the White House. She wanted people to know about the special history of the things they saw. She even gave a tour of the White House on television. More people than ever came to visit the president's home.

Jackie had always loved art, music, and

books. Now, she wanted to make sure these things became a part of the Kennedy presidency. She and Jack invited famous people from all over the world to perform at the White House. Pablo Casals was a famous Spanish musician. He made a special trip to the White House to play the cello for President and Mrs. Kennedy. Carl Sandburg, an important American poet, came to recite some of his poems. Rudolf Nureyev, a Russian-born ballet dancer, and Roberta Peters, an American opera singer, also performed at the White House.

Americans were happy to have so many talented men and women visit the White House. They felt that Jackie had helped to make Washington a bright and interesting place.

People outside the United States started noticing the First Lady, too. In May of 1961,

Jackie traveled to Paris with President Kennedy. Everywhere they went, huge crowds waited to see Jackie. They liked the beautiful young woman who spoke French so well.

At a dinner with General Charles de Gaulle, the president of France, Jackie translated for her husband and de Gaulle. De Gaulle thought that Jackie was charming and smart. He told President Kennedy, "Your wife knows more French history than most French women."

President Kennedy was very proud of his wife. When they left France, he joked about how she had outshined him. He said, "I am the man who accompanied Jacqueline Kennedy to Paris—and I have enjoyed it."

The president knew that people liked and respected Jackie. They listened to what she had to say. Sometimes Jackie traveled on her own to meet with government officials from other countries. Some of the places she visited without President Kennedy were India, Pakistan, Italy, and the countries of Latin America. Everywhere she went, Jackie helped to keep a feeling of good will between the United States and the country she was visiting.

In 1963, Jackie decided to cut down on her traveling. She and Jack were expecting another baby. On August 7, 1963, their baby boy was born. Jackie and Jack named him Patrick Bouvier Kennedy.

From the moment Patrick was born, Jackie and Jack were very worried about him. The baby was tiny. He weighed just four pounds. And he was very sick. He had trouble breathing. When he was only two days old, Patrick Kennedy died.

Jackie was very sad about losing her baby

son. But she was grateful that she still had Jack, Caroline, and John-John. She told her husband, "The one blow I could not bear would be to lose you."

John Kennedy worked hard during his presidency. He talked to leaders from many different countries about keeping peace in the world. He worked to make laws that would help poor people and old people. But there were more things the president wanted to do.

President Kennedy was already thinking about the next election, which would take place in 1964. Jack intended to run for president again. The election was still a year away, but Jack was ready to start campaigning. He wanted people to know how much he had done since becoming president. And he wanted to tell them about his plans for the future.

In the fall of 1963, Jack planned a trip to

Dallas, Texas. Jackie decided to go with him.

President and Mrs. Kennedy arrived in Dallas on November 22. They rode through the streets of the city in an open car. The Secret Service men guarding the president wanted to put a bulletproof top over the car. President Kennedy refused. He wanted to be closer to the people who came to greet him.

The governor of Texas, John Connally, and his wife rode in the same car with the Kennedys. As the car drove through the streets of Dallas, crowds of people waved and cheered. President Kennedy and Jackie waved back.

Suddenly, rifle shots rang out. The president had been shot!

A few minutes later, President Kennedy was dead.

The people of the United States had lost

their president. And Jackie Kennedy had lost her husband.

Jackie was just 34 years old. She said: "I should have known that it was asking too much to dream that I might have grown old with him and see our children grow up together."

Jackie was especially sad that her children had lost their father. Caroline was only six years old. John-John had just turned three.

The children had not had a chance to say good-bye to their father before he died. Jackie wanted to give them that chance. She asked her son and daughter to write to their father in heaven.

John-John did not yet know how to write. He scribbled and drew on a sheet of paper. Caroline wrote her father a note. It read: "Dear Daddy, We're all going to miss you. Daddy I love you very much. Caroline."

9

After JFK

After John F. Kennedy was killed, Lyndon Johnson was sworn in as the new president. President Johnson and his family moved into the White House. Jackie, Caroline, and John-John had to find a new place to live.

At first, Jackie decided to stay in Washington. Before the Kennedys had moved into the White House, they had lived in a neighborhood called Georgetown. Jackie decided that she and her children would move back there.

Now newspaper reporters paid even more attention to Jackie and her children. They camped outside their house night and day. Anytime Jackie, Caroline, or John-John went anywhere, reporters followed. They asked many questions and took pictures.

Jackie wanted to be left alone. She tried to ignore the reporters. But she could not find any privacy for her family. Finally, Jackie decided to move someplace where they would not always be in the public eye.

That place was New York City. In 1964, Jackie, Caroline, and John-John moved into an apartment on Fifth Avenue. Jackie liked living in the city. Central Park was right across the street. Jackie's sister, Lee, lived down the block. Jackie was especially happy that reporters could not enter her building. No one could bother her or the children when they were at home.

In the fall, Caroline started second grade at a Catholic school called the Convent of the Sacred Heart. John Jr. entered kindergarten a year later. He went to St. David's School.

Caroline and John Jr. always knew that their mother was there for them. Jackie never missed one of their school plays or recitals. They came to her with their homework. And she helped them with their horseback-riding lessons.

Jackie had never stopped riding horses. Now Caroline and John Jr. were learning to ride, too. Caroline's horse was named Macaroni. Jackie taught Caroline and John Jr. to sit straight when they rode. She showed them how to keep their heels down in the stirrups.

Jackie wanted her children to do the same fun things as other kids. She took Caroline and John-John to the circus and to the New

On vacation in Ireland, Jackie and the children enjoy a day of horseback riding.

York World's Fair. They went rowing in Central Park. Jackie took her son and daughter on vacations to Hawaii and Switzerland.

Caroline, John Jr., and their mother did not lose touch with the Kennedy family. They still visited Jack's mother and father, Rose and Joe Kennedy. Jack had had five brothers and sisters with whom they were still close. These aunts and uncles were all married and had lots of children. Caroline and John Jr. liked to play with all of their cousins. They had fun together.

Jackie still enjoyed traveling. During a trip to Greece, she met a man named Aristotle Onassis. Most people called him Ari. Ari owned a big shipping company in Greece. He was very rich. He lived on his own private island called Skorpios.

Ari was 23 years older than Jackie. He was short and had a big belly. Sometimes his clothes were rumpled. But Jackie liked him. She and Ari talked about getting married.

A lot of people did not want Jackie to marry Ari Onassis. They thought that he was too old for her. They remembered Jack

*Jackie and Aristotle Onassis get married
on the island of Skorpios.*

Kennedy, and they did not think that this man was handsome enough or stylish enough.

Jackie decided to marry Ari anyway. Their wedding was on Skorpios, on October 20, 1968. Caroline and John Jr. were there. Ari's son and daughter were at the wedding, too. Their names were Alexander and Christina.

After the wedding, Jackie and her children moved to Greece to be with Ari. They lived on Skorpios. Jackie was glad to leave the United States. She was afraid that she and her children were not safe there now.

Something terrible had happened to make Jackie afraid. In June of 1968, Jack's brother Bobby Kennedy had been killed. Bobby had decided to run for president of the United States. While he was campaigning in California, a man named Sirhan Sirhan shot Bobby.

Jackie was very upset by Bobby's death. First Jack had been killed. Now Bobby. Jackie worried that Caroline and John Jr. might be next. "If they are killing Kennedys, my kids are number-one targets," she said.

In Greece, Jackie felt safer. She and her family had privacy on Skorpios. Security guards were with Jackie and her children wherever they went.

Ari liked to give Jackie, Caroline, and John Jr. presents. Sometimes he would leave Jackie a bracelet or a poem on her breakfast tray. He gave John Jr. a real speedboat and a jukebox. He gave Caroline her own sailboat.

But after a few years, Jackie and Ari started to grow apart. They had problems in their marriage. Jackie still had her apartment in New York City. She began spending more and more time there. Ari was busy with work. He and Jackie did not see each other very often. People began to wonder if they would get divorced.

In the end, Jackie and Ari Onassis were not divorced. Early in 1975, Ari became very ill. On March 15, he died. Ari was buried on Skorpios, near the same chapel where he and Jackie had been married.

Jackie was now a widow for the second

time. She was only 45 years old. Once again, she had to think about what she would do next.

"I have always lived through men," Jackie said. First she had been the wife of a president of the United States. Then she had been the wife of a very wealthy businessman.

Jackie was no longer anyone's wife. She wanted to start living for herself.

10
The New Jackie O

Jacqueline Kennedy Onassis was now a very wealthy woman. After Ari's death, Jackie had over $20 million. She could do whatever she wanted.

What Jackie wanted to do was to get a job.

Jackie had always been interested in art, music, and ballet. And she had always loved books. She decided to work for a company where she could help to publish books about the things that she loved.

Working hard as a book editor at Viking Press.

First, Jackie worked for a publishing company called Viking Press. A few years later, she joined another company, Doubleday.

The people she worked with were very nervous at the beginning. What would it be like to work with Jackie? Would she be treated differently from everyone else because she was famous? Would Jackie make a good book editor?

Jackie worked in an office that was small and cramped. She made her own coffee, just like everyone else. She dressed very casually. Sometimes she sat cross-legged on the floor of her office to work.

"Initially we were in awe," said one of Jackie's coworkers. "We'd say, 'Gosh, she came to our floor, and she's in stretch pants.'"

Steven Rubin, the president of Doubleday, was very impressed with Jackie. He said: "She had this tremendous enthusiasm when she talked about a book. Every single person on the staff adored her. She really connected with the authors, too. She was warm, engaging, smart—a friend."

An editor who worked with Jackie said: "She really liked to work on manuscripts and put books together. She had a flair for it and worked hard at it."

What exactly did Jackie do?

Jackie knew many famous men and women. She thought that other people would want to read about their lives and work. She asked artists, musicians, and dancers to write about what they did. She read their stories and gave them advice. She helped the authors organize the things they wanted to say. Jackie even helped decide how each book would look and what would go on the cover.

Jackie convinced singer Michael Jackson to write a book about himself. It was called *Moonwalk*. She worked on a children's book with the singer Carly Simon. Jackie asked a famous ballerina named Gelsey Kirkland to tell her life story, too. She worked on a book about former French president Charles de Gaulle. Another book she worked on was about the life of the famous singer and song-writer John Lennon.

Jackie felt that each of her books was very special. She said: "To me, a wonderful book is one that takes me on a journey into something I didn't know before." One of the things she loved about her work was that she was not the center of attention. Everyone focused mainly on the books themselves and the people who wrote them.

The authors who worked with Jackie liked her enthusiasm. They felt that she helped them to write the best books possible. A man named Jonathan Cott wrote books about ancient Egypt that Jackie edited. He said: "She was intelligent and passionate about the material. She was an ideal reader and an ideal editor."

Another writer said, "When Jackie got enthusiastic, you thought she was going to burst into song."

Jackie became involved in other projects as well. She was happy to be living and working in New York City. She felt that it was a wonderful city. It has many beautiful old buildings. Jackie thought the old buildings gave New York City a feeling all its own.

But New York City was changing. Shiny new skyscrapers were being built all the time. In 1975, Jackie learned of a plan to build a tall skyscraper right above Grand Central Terminal. Jackie did not want the skyscraper to be built. Grand Central was one of her favorite old buildings. The front of the station was made of beautiful carved stone. Jackie thought that the new building would spoil the look of Grand Central. People would not be able to appreciate what a special place it was.

Jackie spoke out against the new tower. She even traveled to Washington, D.C., to

Jackie strives to preserve Grand Central Terminal as a historic landmark.

tell people in the federal government why she thought building the skyscraper was a bad idea. People all over New York began to hear about the struggle to save Grand Central Terminal. They sent money to support Jackie's cause.

In the end, Jackie's fight was a success. The skyscraper was not built.

Jackie did not stop there. Another tall office tower was planned. This one would be right next to a church called St. Bartholomew's. Jackie thought that the new building would ruin the special feeling of the old church. She went to Albany, the capital of New York State, with other people who felt the same way. They spoke to the governor and other politicians. People listened to Jackie. She and her friends won that fight, too.

Jackie found time for another cause that was important to her. Her friend Rosey Grier had started a program to help poor children who lived in the inner city. It was called "Giant Step." Jackie helped to raise money for Giant Step. She visited boys and girls who lived in a poor neighborhood in Los Angeles. She hoped that she could give them hope for their lives.

Now, Jackie's days were filled with work that she loved. Every morning when she got up, she went jogging around the reservoir in Central Park. Three days a week, she worked at Doubleday book publishers. On the days she wasn't at the office, she devoted time to her other causes.

To relax, she practiced yoga and rode horses. Jackie had built a home on Martha's Vineyard, a pretty island off the coast of Massachusetts. She, Caroline, and John Jr. liked to go there on weekends and vacations. Jackie also had a home in Bernardsville, New Jersey, where she rode horses.

Jackie Kennedy Onassis was living her life exactly the way she wanted.

11
Family Life

The most important thing to Jackie was her family. She once said: "I want John and Caroline to grow up to be good people."

Jackie was always there for Caroline and John Jr., even during the hardest times. She held a birthday party for John Jr. on the night of President Kennedy's funeral. Jackie knew how important birthdays are to little boys. She would not think of canceling John-John's party.

Jackie worried about her children growing up without a father. She wanted to make sure that they were strong and independent. She wanted them to study and work hard. She taught them to care about other people.

When Caroline was a teenager, she went to the Appalachian Mountains to learn about the mining families who lived there. John Jr. went to Guatemala to help people whose homes had been destroyed by an earthquake. He also joined a leadership program, where he learned how to survive on his own in the outdoors.

After college, both Caroline and John Jr. decided to go to law school. Caroline went to Columbia University School of Law. John Jr. attended New York University Law School.

In 1981, Caroline met a man named Edwin Schlossberg. Ed is 13 years older than Caroline. He is smart and artistic. He helped design the Brooklyn Children's Museum.

John Jr.'s graduation from New York
University Law School.

Caroline thought he was funny and caring. They were married on July 19, 1986.

As a lawyer, Caroline co-wrote an article, "In Our Defense—The Bill of Rights in Action." After John Jr. graduated from law school, he went to work as an assistant district attorney in Manhattan. He helped to prepare cases against men and women being tried in the courts for serious crimes. In 1988, he introduced Senator Ted Kennedy when he spoke at the Democratic National Convention.

Jackie was proud of Caroline and John Jr. She was pleased that they might be following in their father's footsteps by choosing legal careers. Perhaps they would go into politics. Most of all, she wanted them to be happy. She said that helping her children to become happy adults was "the best thing I have ever done."

Jackie, Caroline, and John Jr. continued to make public appearances that were important to them and their family. In 1979, they attended the dedication of the John F. Kennedy Presidential Library in Boston. In 1988, they participated in events commemorating the twenty-fifth anniversary of President Kennedy's assassination. Jackie and her children also went to special performances at the John F. Kennedy Center for the Performing Arts, in Washington, D.C.

That year was a very exciting one for Jackie. She became a grandmother! On June 25, 1988, Caroline gave birth to a baby daughter. She and Ed named the little girl Rose Kennedy Schlossberg, after Jack Kennedy's mother.

Two years later, Caroline and Ed had another daughter. Her name is Tatiana Celia Kennedy Schlossberg. And in 1993, they had a son. They named him John Bouvier Kennedy Schlossberg, after both Caroline's father and Jackie's father.

Jackie loved being a grandmother. Once a week, she baby-sat for Rose, Tatiana, and little Jack. She liked to play with them in Central Park. Jackie would buy her grand-

*Rose and Tatiana enjoy a carousel ride
with their grandmother.*

children ice cream cones and cotton candy. She took them for rides on the merry-go-round. It was the same merry-go-round Caroline and John-John had ridden on when they were little!

Jackie's family was growing. In addition to having her children and grandchildren,

Jackie had become friends with a man who felt just like family. His name was Maurice Tempelsman.

Maurice was a diamond merchant who had known the Kennedys for years. He was charming and lively, and Jackie loved being with him. She and Maurice shared many interests. They both enjoyed reading, traveling, and going to the opera. They liked being outdoors. Maurice became Jackie's closest companion.

Jackie's greatest joy—spending time with her family.
Here she is in Central Park with Caroline,
grandson John, and Maurice Tempelsman.

Jackie had been through some hard times. Her parents had had a bitter divorce. Her first husband had been killed. Her second husband had died while she and her children were still young. Newspaper reporters hounded her for years.

Now, things were peaceful for Jackie. She was happy. She looked forward to growing older with her family and friends nearby. Most of all, she was excited about watching Rose, Tatiana, and Jack grow up.

12

The End of an Era

One day, at the beginning of 1994, Jackie went to see her doctor. She thought she had a cold. But the doctor told her that she had a more serious illness. It was called non-Hodgkin's lymphoma.

Non-Hodgkin's lymphoma is a type of cancer. It attacks a person's immune system. When that happens, it is very hard for the sick person to fight off other illnesses. The cancer can spread throughout the body. It cannot always be cured.

Jackie and President Bill Clinton share a warm moment.

Jackie's doctors told her that her disease had not spread very far. They gave her drugs to kill the cancer. Jackie began a special treatment called chemotherapy. Everyone thought there was a good chance that she would get well.

Jackie did not want to change anything in her life just because she was sick. She continued working at Doubleday. She still baby-sat for Rose, Tatiana, and Jack. She took walks in Central Park and went to the movies with friends.

But she did not get well. The treatment for Jackie's non-Hodgkin's lymphoma did not work. Before long, the cancer spread to her brain and to her liver. By the middle of May, Jackie was very, very sick. She went to the hospital, but the doctors could not do anything to save her.

Jackie did not want to spend her last days in the hospital. She wanted to be at home with her family.

Caroline and John Jr. brought their mother home. They and Maurice Tempelsman stayed by her side day and night. Close friends and relatives came to be with Jackie and say good-bye. Jack Kennedy's brother, Senator Ted Kennedy, flew up from Washington, D.C. The priest from Jackie's church visited, too.

On the evening of May 19, 1994, Jacqueline Kennedy Onassis died.

"She was surrounded by her friends and family and her books and the people and the things she loved," John Jr. told the grieving crowd of people outside Jackie's apartment. "And now she's in God's hands."

The day after Jackie's death, hundreds of people stood outside her apartment building. They cried and shouted, "We love Jackie." Other people left flowers there and at the front gate of her house on Martha's Vineyard. At the John F. Kennedy Library, in Boston, more than 500 people came to see a painting of Jackie. They signed their names in a memorial book beneath the painting. People signed another book in Grand Central Terminal. They wanted Jackie's relatives to know how sad they were that the world had lost such a wonderful, brave woman.

Caroline and John Jr. mourn the loss of their beloved mother and friend.

Caroline and John Jr. decided to give a special name to the reservoir in Central Park where their mother liked to jog. It is now called Lake Jackie.

Men and women around the world were sad to hear about Jackie's death. "In times of hope, she captured our hearts," said

Lady Bird Johnson, the widow of President Lyndon Johnson. "She was an image of beauty and romance and leaves an empty place in the world."

Former President Jimmy Carter said: "She showed us how one could approach tragedy with courage."

Jackie had always been a private person. Caroline and John Jr. wanted to respect her privacy even after her death. They decided not to allow the public or the press to attend the funeral service at Jackie's church.

On May 23, Jackie was buried next to John F. Kennedy in Arlington National Cemetery. Members of her family came to pay their respects to Jackie. Close friends and politicians from around the world came, too. The bells at Washington National Cathedral rang 64 times—once for each year of Jackie's life.

An American legend.

President Bill Clinton spoke at Jackie's burial service. "God gave her very great gifts and imposed upon her great burdens," he said. "She bore them all with dignity and grace and uncommon common sense."

Senator Ted Kennedy summed up the way many people felt about Jackie. He said: "She graced our history. And for those of us who knew her, she graced our lives."

ANNE CAPECI has written numerous books for children. She has also edited biographies of Amelia Earhart, Martin Luther King, Jr., Jesse Jackson, Roberto Clemente, and other prominent people. *Meet Jacqueline Kennedy Onassis* is the first biography she has written.

Ms. Capeci lives in Brooklyn, New York.

Bullseye Biographies